Giants
on the
Road

Tanker Trucks

Norman D. Graubart

PowerKiDS press.

New York

Published in 2015 by The Rosen Publishing Group, Inc.
29 East 21st Street, New York, NY 10010

First Edition

Editor: Katie Kawa
Book Design: Jonathan J. D'Rozario

Photo Credits: Cover Lester Lefkowitz/The Image Bank/Getty Images; p. 5 Vibrant Image Studio/Shutterstock.com; pp. 6, 22 majeczka/Shutterstock.com; p. 9 linavita/Shutterstock.com; p. 10 Justin Sullivan/Getty Images News/ Getty Images; p. 13 Stuart Monk/Shutterstock.com; p. 14 Alvis Upitis/Photographer's Choice RF/Getty Images; p. 17 Robert Pernell/Shutterstock.com; p. 18 Vacclav/Shutterstock.com; p. 21 glen gaffney/Shutterstock.com; p. 24 Worldpics/Shutterstock.com.

Library of Congress Cataloging-in-Publication Data

Graubart, Norman D., author.
 Tanker trucks / Norman D. Graubart.
     pages cm. — (Giants on the road)
 Includes bibliographical references and index.
 ISBN 978-1-4994-0261-2 (pbk.)
 ISBN 978-1-4994-0225-4 (6 pack)
 ISBN 978-1-4994-0226-1 (library binding)
 1. Tank trucks—Juvenile literature. I. Title.
 TL230.15.G736 2015
 629.224—dc23
                            2014025308

Manufactured in the United States of America

Contents

Have you ever seen
a tanker truck?
They are very big!

tank

Tanker trucks have large tanks on them. Tanks hold liquids.

A liquid is matter that flows freely. Water is a liquid.

Gasoline is a liquid.
Tanker trucks carry gasoline
to **filling stations**.

Gasoline makes things run.
People put it in cars and trucks.

Some tanker trucks carry foods, such as milk. Some carry water.

Food tanker trucks have to keep the food cold.

Large tanker trucks can hold as much water as 450 bathtubs!

Tanker truck drivers need to drive safely. They have a lot of goods on board!

Next time you see a tanker truck, guess what it's carrying!

Words to Know

filling station

Index

Websites

Due to the changing nature of Internet links, PowerKids Press has developed an online list of websites related to the subject of this book. This site is updated regularly. Please use this link to access the list: www.powerkidslinks.com/gotr/tatr